PETER'S POCKET

Written by Judi Barrett. Illustrated by Julia Noonan.

Atheneum New York 1974

for PETER adam kringstein

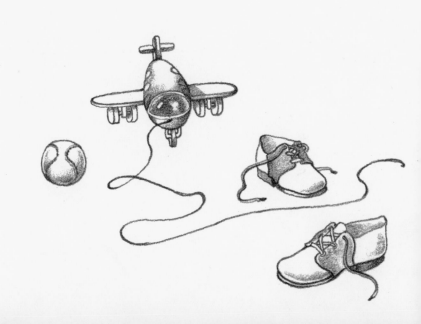

Peter is three and three-quarters years old.

Almost four.

He likes to collect
all sorts of things
that he especially likes
and carry them around with him
during the day.

Things like
raisins,

RAISINS
SUN
RIPENED   2 OZ

and nuts,

and picture puzzle pieces,

and marbles,

and finger puppets,

and crayons,

and
small pieces of paper
that he can glue
onto larger pieces of paper,

and pennies

and nickels,

and cookies,

and little toy cars,

and lots of other things.

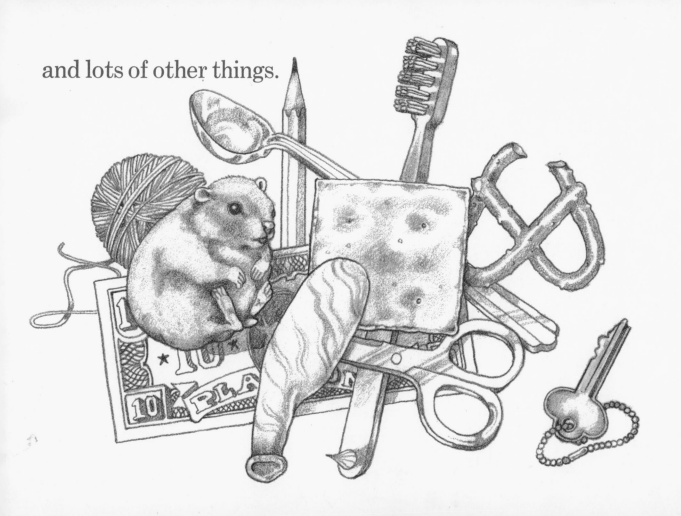

But he couldn't possibly
carry all those things
around in his hands,
so he liked to put them
in his pockets.

Some of Peter's clothing had pockets.

His snow jacket
had three pockets.

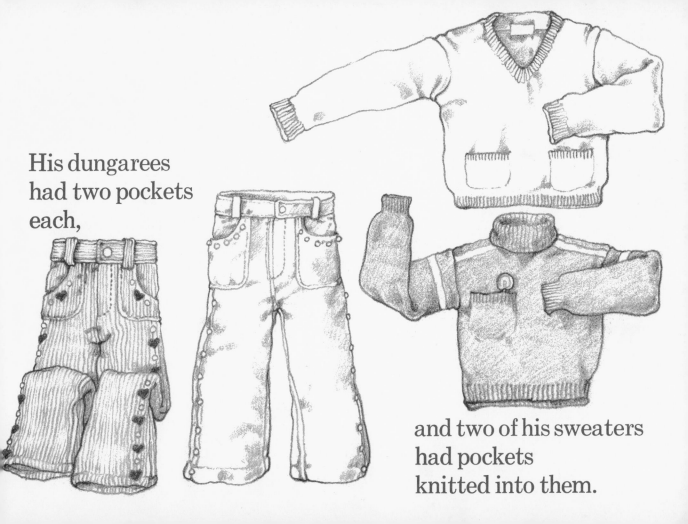

His dungarees
had two pockets
each,

and two of his sweaters
had pockets
knitted into them.

But not everything had pockets.

Only one polo shirt
had a pocket.

His plaid pants
had no pockets.

Most of his shorts
didn't have
any pockets.

His bathing suit
had no pockets.

And none
of his pajamas
had any pockets.

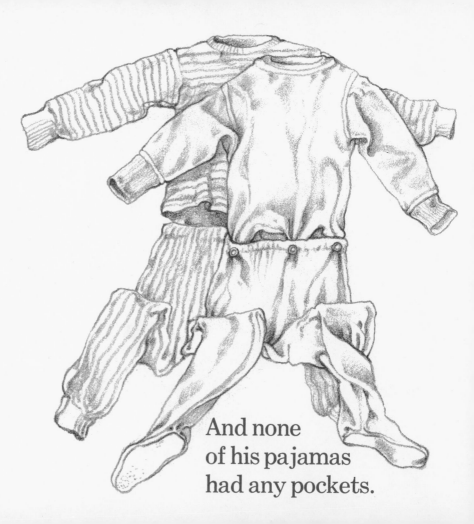

The only clothes
Peter liked to wear
were the ones
with pockets in them.

But there never
seemed to be
enough pockets
for Peter
on anything he wore.

Peter's mother
thought of a wonderful idea.
Portable pin-on pockets.
Pockets that could be safety-pinned
onto anything Peter was wearing,
at any time.
They could even be moved around
without emptying them out.

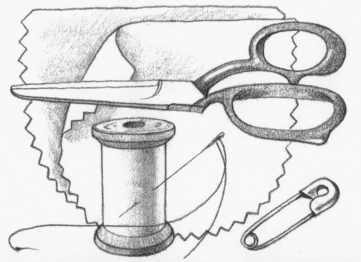

So, she cut the pockets
out of material,
sewed them up,
and wrote 'Peter's Pocket'
on each one.

Peter had pockets on everything now.

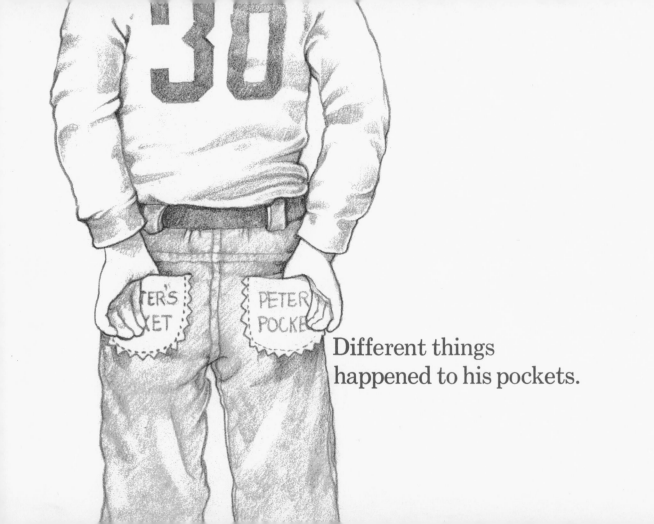

Different things
happened to his pockets.

Raisins
made them
sticky.

PETER'S
POCKET

Cookies
made them
crumby.

Crayons
made them different colors
inside.

Pencils
made holes in them
sometimes.

His ball stuffed up
the pocket.

Pennies and nickels
made his pocket
feel heavy.

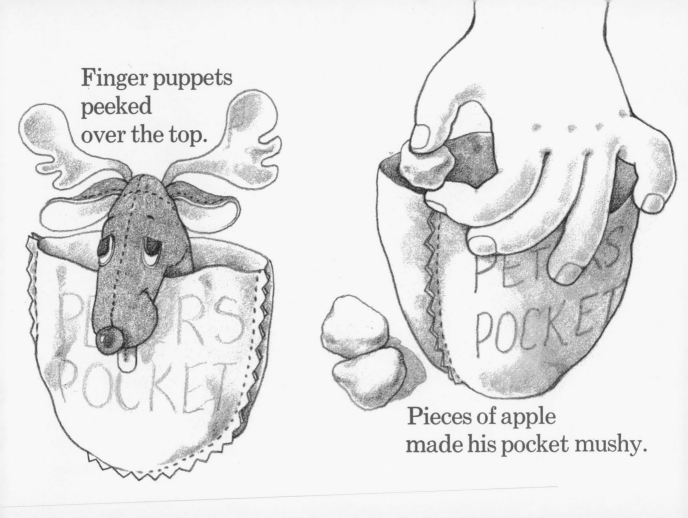

Finger puppets
peeked
over the top.

Pieces of apple
made his pocket mushy.

Toy cars
made a lot
of little bumps.

And an ice cube
made a
cold lump

until it began
to melt.

Then the pocket
got all wet.

Sometimes
Peter could tell
what was in the pocket
by feeling the outside.

Other times
he had to put his hand in
to remember
what he had put
inside.

Peter liked finding things in the pockets.

He could also just keep his hands
in his pockets.

When the pockets wore out,

his mother
sewed him new ones.

And when they got really dirty,

she just washed them out,

and hung them up to dry.

Then they were all ready
to be filled up again.

Instructions for making Peter's Pocket

1. Cut two patterns for each pocket, using a pinking shears except on the top edge.

2. Put pieces together and sew on the dotted line.

3. Attach a safety pin.

4. Fill your pocket.

A Pattern for Peter's Pocket

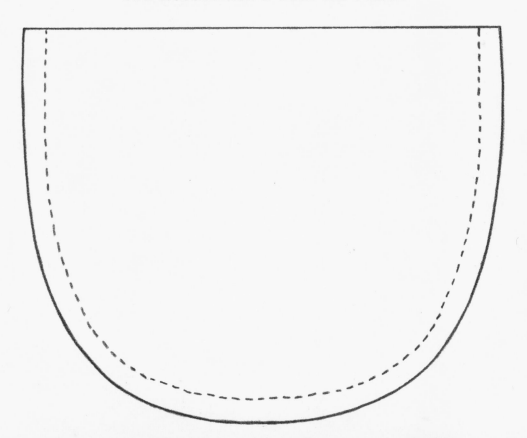